To Anna + Rachel,
... with lots of love.
June 2023.

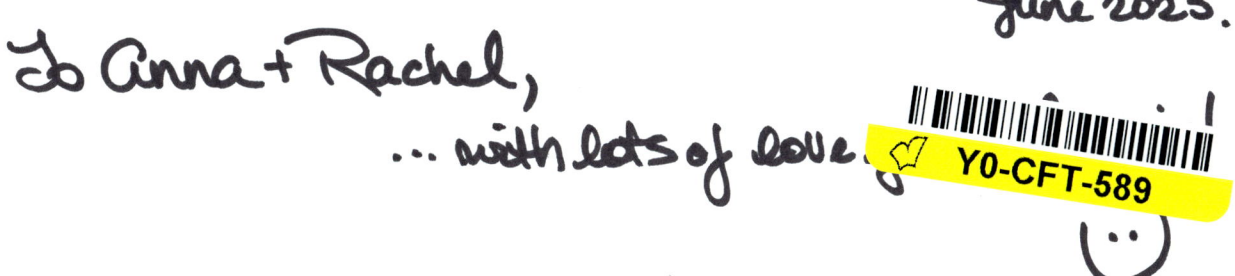

Lizzie and the Man in the Moon

Written by Liz MacRae

Illustrated by Kim Rumbolt

To Anna + Rachel,
.. with lots of love from Tizzie!
:)

June 2023.

Thank you Andrea Sadler for

saying this story would make a lovely book,

and to Samara O'Gorman who led me to Kim,

whose illustrations are so charming!

Thank you too to Tony Robbins,

a great and wonderful teacher.

Lizzie sat by herself on a bench by an empty soccer field near her home.

She looked up at the moon.
The Man in the Moon was crying.

He said they are too proud when they say "I'm so busy!", as if it is a badge of some measure of success.

Lizzie told him, "I've said I'm so busy hundreds of times!"

He said, "I know, I've heard you from way up here."

He smiled at her through his tears, but tears still fell.

Lizzie asked him if he wanted to talk about it.

She wouldn't like to leave someone alone and crying.

She gave him a virtual hug.

The Man in the Moon said that he longed

for the day when humans would

smile at each other and happily say,

"I'm so balanced."

He remarked

how both

busy

and

balanced

begin with a b, and that

the meanings are so far apart.

He said that we need to be more loving to one another,

more quiet, more interested in listening to each other.

We must

respond,

not

react.

Love must be the first thing we think of

before we open our mouths to speak to anyone.

The Man in the Moon said, "You are all in this together. Some of you are right."

Lizzie asked him, "Who is right? Tell me, please."

He replied, "That, I cannot tell you. Time will tell you. Like I said, you are all in this together. You all need to figure this out. I will give you a hint though."

As he whispered his hint to her, a train passed nearby at that very same moment.

Lizzie thought she heard him say, *"Love each other."*

Yes, she was pretty sure that's what he said.

They sat a few more minutes in silence.

Lizzie left the soccer field feeling happy that she'd made a new friend.

The Man in the Moon followed her home

and made sure she got safely inside her house.

Such a gentleman.

Story copyright © 2023 by Liz MacRae.
Illustrations © 2023 by Kim Rumbolt.

All rights reserved. No part of this publication may be reproduced, stored in a retrieval system, or transmitted, in any form or by any means, electronic, mechanical, photocopying, recording or otherwise, without the written prior permission of the author.

ISBN: 9798377775034

Manufactured by Amazon.ca
Bolton, ON